Rosen, Michael J.

With a Dog like that
a kid like me...

With a Dog Like That, a Kid Like Me...

Michael J. Rosen
pictures by Ted Rand

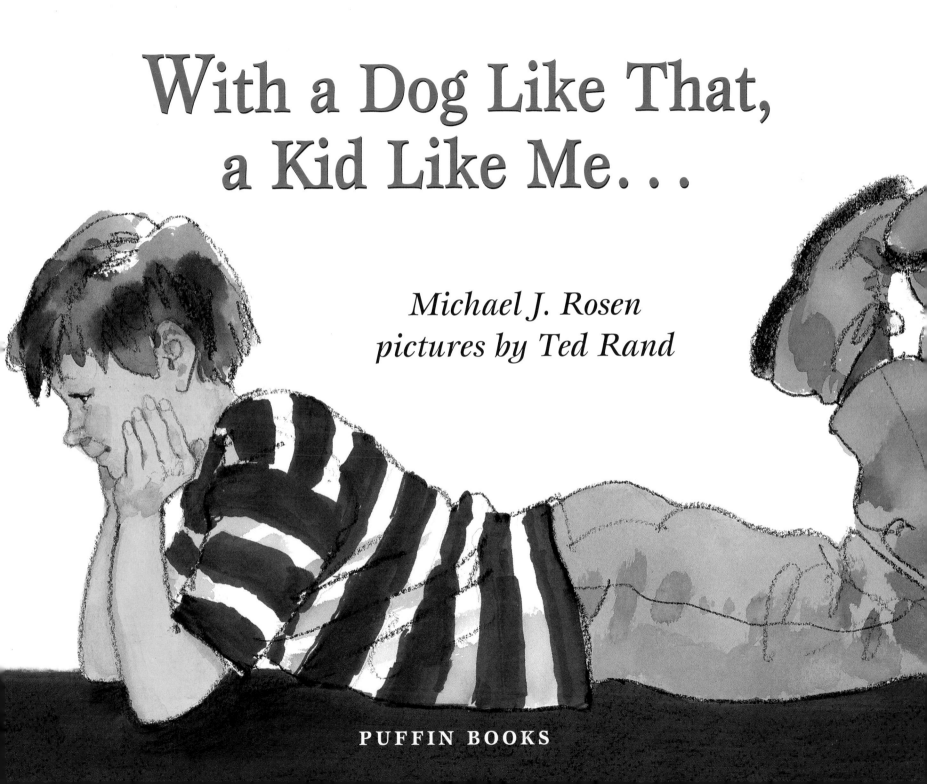

PUFFIN BOOKS

PUFFIN BOOKS
Published by the Penguin Group
Penguin Putnam Books for Young Readers,
345 Hudson Street, New York, New York 10014, U.S.A.
Penguin Books Ltd, 80 Strand, London WC2R ORL, England
Penguin Books Australia Ltd, Ringwood, Victoria, Australia
Penguin Books Canada Ltd, 10 Alcorn Avenue, Toronto, Ontario, Canada M4V 3B2
Penguin Books (N.Z.) Ltd, 182-190 Wairau Road, Auckland 10, New Zealand

Penguin Books Ltd, Registered Offices: Harmondsworth, Middlesex, England

First published in the United States of America by Dial Books for Young Readers,
a division of Penguin Putnam Inc., 2000
Published by Puffin Books, a division of Penguin Putnam Books for Young Readers, 2002

1 3 5 7 9 10 8 6 4 2

THE LIBRARY OF CONGRESS HAS CATALOGUED THE DIAL EDITION AS FOLLOWS:
Rosen, Michael J., date.
With a dog like that, a kid like me . . . /by Michael J. Rosen
pictures by Ted Rand.
p. cm.
Summary: In the eyes of an imaginative boy, his dog becomes a seal when he is slick with soap,
a billy goat when he chews the mail, a croc when he crouches beneath the table stalking a crumb,
and other animals.
ISBN: 0-8037-2059-9
[1. Dogs—Fiction. 2. Animals—Fiction. 3. Imagination—Fiction.]
I. Rand, Ted, ill. II. Title.
PZ7.R71867Wi 2000 [E]—dc21 98-53362 CIP AC

Puffin Books ISBN 0-14-230130-2

Printed in the United States of America

For Paris—our first and forever dog
M.J.R.

To my grandson Roy Willis Rand
T.R.

My Dog

is a purebred golden retriever.

But that doesn't keep

him from being...

a *Pony*

whenever he prances around the yard

with a stick

a Seal

when he's slick with soap

from a sudsy shampoo

_a_ **Kangaroo**

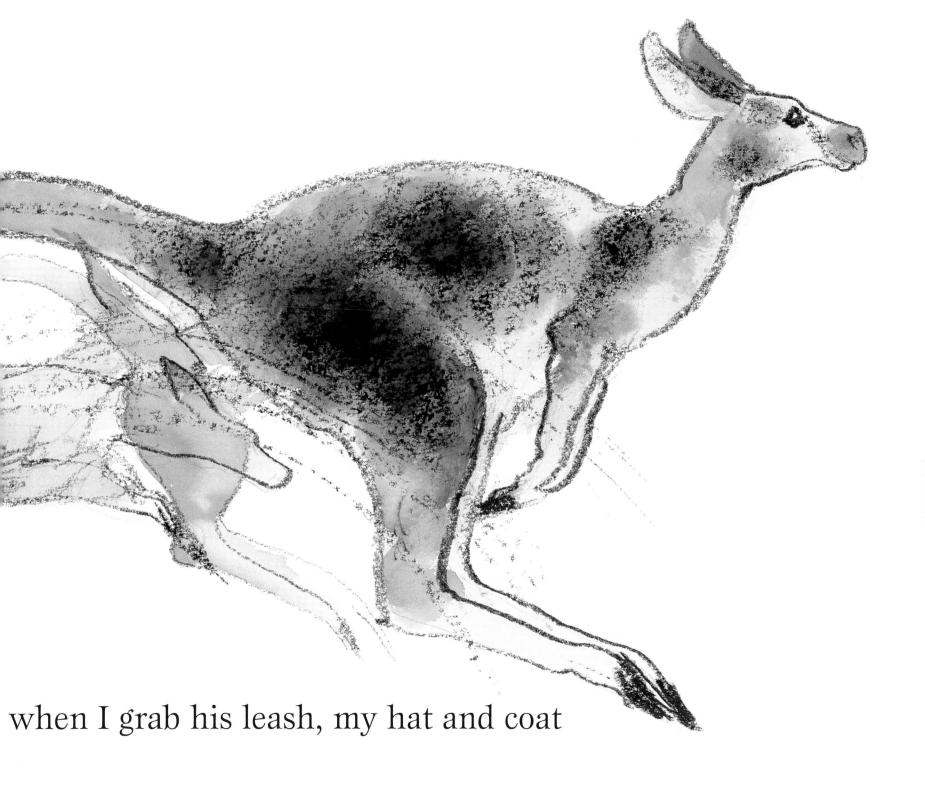

when I grab his leash, my hat and coat

a Billy goat

when he chews the mail
(oh no, not again!)

a *Lion*

in his den when he guards the gate and growls

a Grazing Cow

when he munches grass that hasn't been mowed

a Mole

when he burrows beneath the pillows on the couch

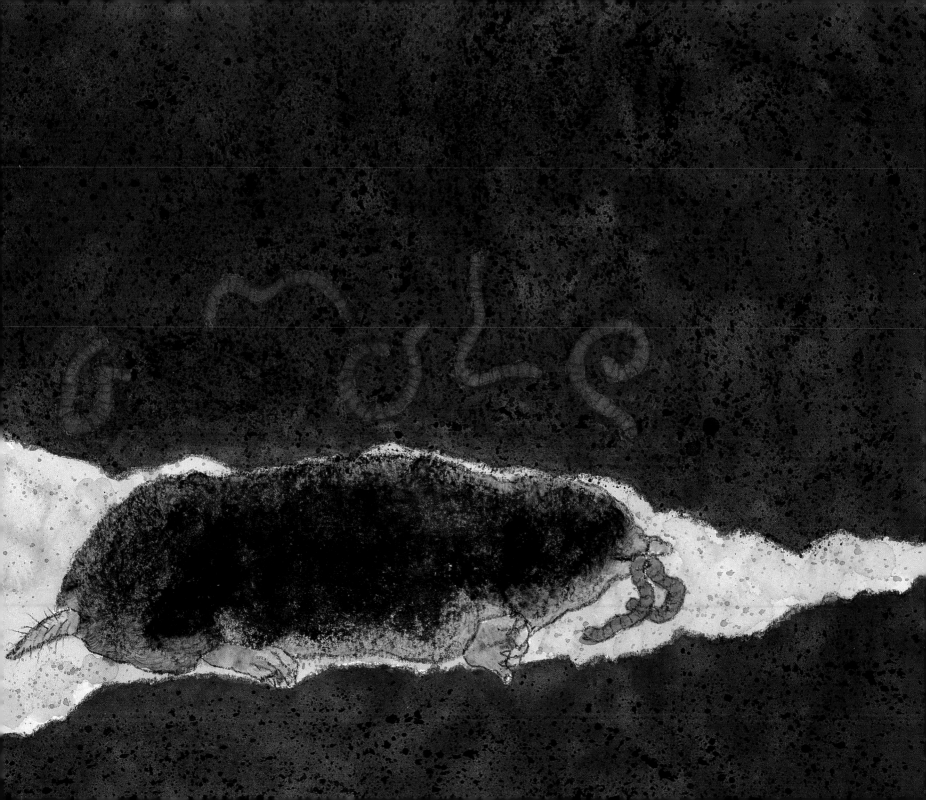

a Croc

when he crouches

beneath the table stalking crumbs

a *Beaver* whenever he

carries a branch as he swims along

a *Groundhog*

when he sits up for me
to scratch his fur

a *Hibernating Bear*

when he naps beside me in bed.

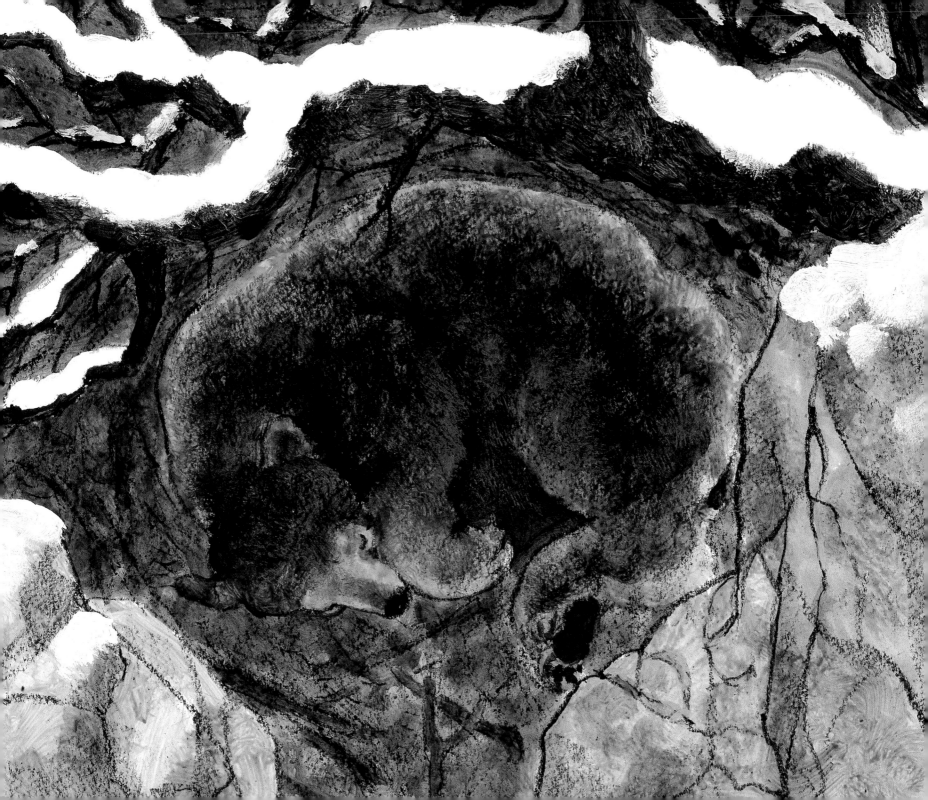

And so, with a dog like *that*, a kid like *me* . . .

can be anything I truly want to be.